PIGS APLENTY, PIGS GALORE!

DAVID McPHAIL

Dutton Children's Books   New York

Library of Congress Cataloging-in-Publication Data

McPhail, David M.

Pigs aplenty, pigs galore! / by David McPhail.—1st ed.

p.   cm.

Summary: Pigs galore invade a house and have a wonderful party.

ISBN 0-525-45079-3

[1. Pigs—Fiction.   2. Stories in rhyme.]   I. Title.

PZ8.3.M4615Pi   1993

[E]—dc20   92-27986   CIP   AC

Published in the United States 1993 by Dutton Children's Books,
a division of Penguin Books USA Inc.

375 Hudson Street, New York, New York 10014

Designed by Riki Levinson

Printed in Hong Kong by South China Printing Co.

First Edition   10 9 8 7 6 5 4 3 2 1

For Jack,
good friend, true poet

Munch Munch Munch

Slurp Slurp Slurp

Crunch Crunch Crunch

Burp Burp Burp

Late one night
As I sat reading,
I thought I heard
The sound of feeding.

Through the kitchen door
I crept,
Barely watching
Where I stepped.

A crash, a bang,
A shout, a yell—
I slipped on something,
Then I fell.

I landed on
A pile of pigs—
Some eating dates,
Some eating figs.

In the cupboards,
On the floor—
Pigs aplenty,
Pigs galore!

Black pigs, white pigs,
Brown and pink pigs,
Making-oatmeal-
In-the-sink pigs.

Pigs in tutus,
Pigs in kilts,
Pigs on skateboards,
Pigs on stilts.

Pigs from England,
Pigs from France,
Pigs in just
Their underpants.

The King of Pigs,
The Piggy Queen—
The biggest pigs
I've ever seen.

Pigs arrive
By boat, by plane.
A bus pulls up
And then a train.

A band strikes up.
A piggy sings.
Then, at ten
The doorbell rings.

Someone yells:
"The pizza's here!"
And all the pigs
Begin to cheer.

Flying pizzas
Fill the air.
One goes SPLAT!
Against my chair.

The piggy piggies
Eat their fill.
I get nothing,
Just the bill.

"I've had enough!"
I scream and shout.
"Get out, you pigs!
You pigs, get out!"

"Please let us stay,"
  The piggies cry.
"Don't make us go,
  Don't say good-bye."

"You can stay,"
  I tell them all.
"But sweep the floor
  And scrub the wall."

I give them brooms,
A pail, a mop.
"Now sweep and scrub
Till I say stop."

The piggies work
And when they're done,
Upstairs they stagger
One by one.

They brush their teeth
And comb their tails,
Then wash their snouts
And clean their nails.

The pigs and I
Climb into bed.
I plump the pillows,
Plop my head.

I close my eyes
And try to sleep.
Before too long
I'm dreaming deep—

Of pigs and pigs
And pigs some more—
Of pigs aplenty,
Pigs galore!